BOOK STRATEGY MANUAL

Layering Book Writing Through Lasagna

by Sam TheLasagna Lady

Publisher: PIAOTT Publishing LLC, Chicago, IL

Book Strategy Manual

Samantha Peavy

Printed in the United States of America

ISBN: 978-1-7362522-0-8

Photography by: David Broughton

A foundation without love is no foundation at all!

~Samantha Peavy

Dedication

This manual is dedicated to the current, prospective, new, and upcoming authors. To the tablet of your mind, I hope this communication technique of writing a book through the lens of lasagna opens up your imagination, dreams, and adventure.

My decades of journaling, along with notes from my book titled Life Through Lasagna Eyes: The Recipes For Life experiences in this manual, if you allow, will thrust and challenge your writing journey beyond your natural view.

To God, thank you for the insight, love and faithfulness of Your heart and sharing with all of us your perspective from another lens. I give thanks to God for His insight and love. I love you.

And to my husband, (Ouie Gouie) Marlon B. Peavy, I love cooking in the kitchen with you. Thank you for being a prophetic voice in our household. ...Your favorite girl, Samantha Ann.

Sam The Lasagna Lady

Strategy Imagination Word
Lasagna
Word Cheese
Strategy
Lasagna
Cheese
Cheese
Lense Word
Baking
Lense
Onion
Lense
Idea
Lense
Word
Journey
Prophetic
Idea
Journey
Word
God
Idea
Cheese
God
Onion
Baking
Writing
Idea
God
Lense
God
Word
Writing
God
Idea
Onion
God
God
Lense
Prophetic
God
Idea
Noodle
God Writing Word
Lemons
Onion Lemons
Lense
Onion
Baking
Noodle
Idea
Word
Noodle Lasagna
Lemons
Strategy Imagination Baking
Lemons
Lasagna
Noodle
Lasagna
Lasagna
Noodle
Imagination
Noodle
Lemons
Prophetic
Prophetic
Cheese
Lense
Lasagna
Idea
Imagination
Idea
Word
Strategy
Cheese
Cheese
Baking
Strategy
Imagination
Lense
Lense
Lense
Cheese
Journey
Lasagna
Noodle
Lasagna
Idea
Journey
Prophetic
God
Cheese
Onion
Writing
Writing
Idea
Journey
God
Strategy
Prophetic
Onion
Noodle
Prophetic
Writing
Word
Onion
Lemons
Onion
Baking
Noodle
Word
Journey
God
Strategy
Writing
Idea
Lemons
Writing
Idea

adidas

The Thought

Lately, many people have asked me questions about how they should write their book? Others made it personal by asking how do I begin Sam? How did you write yours and can you help me?

I put together a short template to assist you, the reader, and your writing journey after being inundated with more inquiries on the same subject. The Lord led me to write this Book Strategy Manual to help others tap prophetically into their internal thought resource and place the being of those words onto pages.

Layout
The Prophetic Idea
Writing
Publishing
Strategy
Outline
Marketing

How This Manual Work

You are the designer of your books. This manual will show you how to write using a different layering technique I call Life Through Lasagna Eyes. This strategy will help you tap into your inner thoughts to write from an eternal perspective. For instance, "In the beginning, was the Word, the Word was with God, and the Word was God." John 1:1 shows the connection in being.

Every individual, in one form or another, has been impacted by words. John 1:1 is used as a guide to layer your written masterpiece, and definitions are included to help shape your writing framework as an author.

This manual, written in 3 dimensions: Parts One, Two, And Three, starts with "In the beginning was the Word" and ends with "And the Word was God." You will discover unique strategies to apply to your writing style, understand prophetic ideas, rediscover imagination, prepare a timeline, and develop a marketing strategy.

As a bonus, I have added a couple of book formats and recipes from my cookbook titled Cooking with Sam The Lasagna Lady, to be released in 2021.

Cook, Eat, and Laugh Often
~Sam The Lasagna Lady

Contents

Introduction

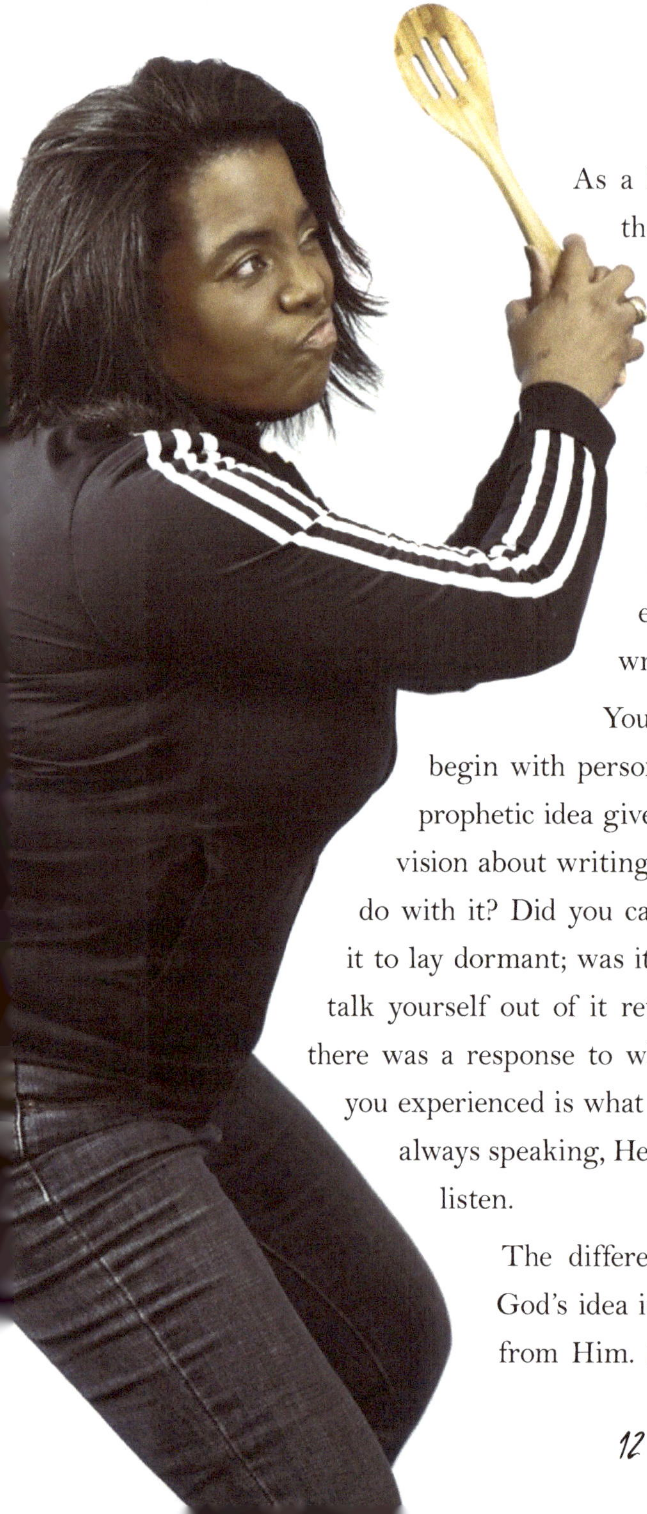

As a little girl, I can not remember the word or dish "lasagna" in my vocabulary. I recall Ravioli's aroma, which is made with pasta, but not quite the same as lasagna. It is funny how one of the world's favorite entrees becomes a beacon for ideas, strategy, or problem-solving, even with a manual on how to write a book.

Your conception of ideas does not begin with personal thoughts. It starts with the prophetic idea given by God. Have you ever had a vision about writing? Think about it. What did you do with it? Did you carry it out, ask questions, allow it to lay dormant; was it cultivated, watered, or did you talk yourself out of it retreating backward. Either way, there was a response to what God is saying. That vision you experienced is what I call a "prophetic idea." God is always speaking, He's speaking right now, but do we listen.

The difference between a good idea and God's idea is that it is prophetic and comes from Him. He invests a "word" or "seed," bringing forth desired results that will yield an increase for His intended purpose. When a gardener plants herbs, there is an expectation for the herbs to harvest. Similar to a prophetic idea that an individual hears and heed to it.

When I layered my first lasagna, thoughts, textures, and ideas flooded my small apartment kitchen. I would recall bizarre foods I tasted over the years and entertained new combinations that I could taste even before developing it. The idea of dining experiences being an answer to many pallets that would embrace any table.

The Bus

Long nights and early mornings fueled the day as I waited anxiously for doors to open and fill my shopping cart with the ingredients of my passion. Ahh, the tomatoes, bell peppers, fresh lean meats, and spices ready for all the clients' orders. Greeted by the business representative's funny jokes and her grounded heart, this brand ambassador made the wait worthwhile.

I loaded my cart full of the needed ingredients and more. So many that the number of items was more than eight bags. Nonetheless, I gathered it with the strength of my heart, passion for lasagna, and pushed my cart towards the bus stop. Upon its arrival, I walked supernaturally, gripping those bags to load on public transportation. I had to make a couple of trips to place the grocery bags full of my passion on the front of the crowded bus.

This book strategy manual includes the joy and anticipation of every bus, train, cab, and later Uber's I had to take to build the character nestled between the layers of my lasagnas. Every grit deserves the "grit" it takes to be resilient beyond circumstances.

Grit Drives Purpose
Samantha Peavy

Life Through Lasagna Eyes

Lasagna fresh out of the oven makes its way to our plates, with each aromatic layer unfolding as it roams through our home. The tomatoes, fresh herbs, pasta, and star ingredients dance in my heart with mouth-watering... Yes, I peeked in the glassed oven door. I heard thunderous clapping, the cheese cheer, and the sauce enjoying the swim of my star ingredient. Lasagna is more than natural ingredients, noodles, and sauces. For me, it is life relatable.

Lenses are a big part of history and continue to evolve. Did you know that Charles Bush's Parlor Kaleidoscope was made in 1873, the heliograph was used to send signals during the French Revolution between 1792-1798, or that the first 3-D Viewer ever made was in 1943? As you can see, lenses grew from being designed to block wind and snow to Ben Franklin's invention of the bifocal. Today we can wear contact lenses directly on our pupils. However, no matter the shape, time frame, or discovery, God is the eternal lens creator. He has a perspective

MOUSE

beyond our natural eyes. This lens is available for anyone to glean from while writing the book from their prophetic idea.

Life through lasagna allows me to balance, have hope, to love, forgive, heal, and thrust forward beyond life's lemons. When I could have chosen hate, God's love within me overshadowed it. His faith guided me when I needed balance; the times I felt like giving up, hope sprung forth.

"Love is patient, love is kind. It does not envy, it does not boast, it is not proud. It does not dishonor others, it is not self-seeking, it is not easily angered, it keeps no records of wrongs. Love does not delight in evil but rejoices with the truth. It always protects, always trusts, always hopes, always perseveres." (1 Corinthians 13:4-7 NIV.)

Love is the ingredient that holds a purpose together. With lasagna, the cheese is a metaphor for that love; it holds the ingredients together. The cheese in your life is the strength needed to help during those lemon moments because it keeps things intact.

When my children were younger in their teens and pre-teens, we would enjoy showing love at the kitchen table. Sometimes, we scattered to the living room. The laughter from the day became medicine for our hearts at the table. Recalling funny stories that served a meaningful purpose allowed us to view things from a different kaleidoscope called lasagna. My children's funny stories, Mason telling Morgan her hair was on fire, Maurice II (Moe-Moe) is such a good kid moment, and Amanda blurting out her first swear word are stories from my book, Life Through Lasagna Eyes: The Recipes For Life. Amanda's first swear word was not the last one she would say. Although I did not hear it, her words were relevant to the point she was making. Hilarious, all the stories created new memories and centered around lasagna.

During a church service, a pastor finished up her sermon. Shortly after, she began to prophesy what God had given her to speak. I can not recall her name, but I can see the light blue robe she wore and her skin's complexion. As she spoke, she began to talk about pasta in detail, and something strange happened to me. I began to feel the weight of the audible words fall on my lap. Now you might be saying, "Okay, Sam, how does that happen?" As she talked, the prophecy was so powerful that I visualized the letters landing individually, forming words as they fell to my lap. Each word became seeds planted in the ground of my heart and took root to grow. Wow, was this refreshing! I was going through many lemons of life; divorce, tragedy, and more.

I liken this to the scripture:

"Behold, I will do a new thing; now it shall spring forth; Shall you not know it? I will even make a road in the wilderness and rivers in the desert. The beast of the field will honor Me, The jackals and the owls, because I gave waters in the wilderness and rivers in the desert, to give drink to My people, my chosen. This people for Myself; they shall declare My praise." (Isaiah 43:19-21 NIV.)

The new thing, roads in the wilderness, waters in the wilderness, and rivers in the desert, is what I was experiencing exactly; my wilderness. If you are going through your wilderness, embrace it.

God is building character within you for his glory. Our beliefs, backgrounds may differ; however, everyone has a seed of purpose.

The question is, will you allow that seed to develop?

The journey of Life's Lasagna broke down character flaws; increased journal writing, fed me when I was hungry, helped me when I was homeless, and carried the weight despite the undulation of ingredients. It also continues to provide for millions of people, both physically and spiritually.

Part One

1

In The Beginning, Was The Word...

After hearing God's Word, have you ever gotten an idea in your mind and pondered on it? What did you do with it? Did you carry out the idea? Maybe you asked questions like how will I do this, what will it take, or I believe what I heard, what is next for a successful implementation of this idea? Perhaps you took another route, choosing to ignore what you heard, allowed it to sit dormant, or embraced other's disbelief of what you heard. Either way, there was a response to what you heard.

This idea from God's Word is what I call a prophetic idea. God is always speaking, but who's listening?

Has anyone ever told you, you should write a book(s)? Did the thought cross your mind before they spoke into your writing journey? Have you contemplated writing a book and then suddenly talked yourself out of it? Did the words of others shape your decision?

I do not profess to be a scholar of divinity; however, I have been regenerated as a new creation in Christ and understand His love for all humanity. Because of this love and a relationship with Him, I can write how prophetic ideas are an alternative way to write a book or manual using my layering technique through lasagna.

WORD

A single distinct meaningful element ....or writing comma use with other words or sometimes alone) To form a sentence and typically shown with a space on the other side when written or printed.

Greek meaning: Translated is "logos."

Logos means "computation," "relation," "law," "rule of conduct," "continuous statement," "discussion," and so on. English words that come close to capturing all the meaning of logos are "explanation," "idea," "concept," or "logic." For a more in-depth definition of this "word" (logos), Strong's Concordance is a good resource to begin.

WORD, translated into the Greek noun Rhema means "that which is spoken," "saying," "the subject of speech," etc. Rhema refers to what is spoken closer to our word "remarks," which is descended from it.

STRATEGY

A plan of action or policy designed to achieve a major or overall aim. The word "strategy" derives from the Greek word stratègos; which derives from two words:

- "Stratos" – meaning army.
- "ago" – which is the ancient Greek for leading/guiding/moving.

IMAGINATION

The faculty or action of forming new ideas, or images or concepts of external objects not present to the senses. The ability of the mind to be creative or resourceful.

Webster's Revised Unabridged Dictionary

1. (n.) The imagine-making power of the mind; the power to create or reproduce; ideally, an object of sense previously

perceived; the power to call up mental imaginations.

2. (n.) The representative power; the power to reconstruct or recombine the materials furnished by direct apprehension; the complex faculty usually termed the plastic or creative power; the fancy.
3. (n.) The power to recombine the materials furnished by experience or memory for the accomplishment of an elevated purpose; the power of conceiving and expressing the ideal.

International Standard Bible Encyclopedia

i-maj-i-na'-shun (yetser, sheriruth; dianoia): "Imagination" is the translation of yetser, properly "a shaping," hence, "a thought."

Greek

5325. phantasia -- imagination, show, display

... imagination, show, display.

Strong's Hebrew

3336. yetser -- a form, framing, purpose

... frame, thing framed, imagination, mind, work. From yatsar; a form; figuratively, conception (i.e., purpose) -- frame, thing framed, imagination, mind, work.

IDEA

A thought or suggestion as to a possible course of action. The aim or purpose.

Webster's Revised Unabridged Dictionary

1. (n.) The transcript, image, or picture of a visible object formed by the mind; also, a similar image of any object whatever, whether sensible or spiritual.
2. (n.) A general notion, or a conception formed by generalization.
3. (n.) Hence: Any object apprehended, conceived, or thought of,

by the mind; a notion, conception, or thought; the real object conceived or thought of.

Greek

2397. idea -- countenance, appearance

... 2396, 2397. idea. 2398 . ... countenance, appearance From eido; a sight (comparative figuratively "idea"), ie Aspect -- countenance. see GREEK eido. ...3056. logos -- a word (as embodying an idea), a statement, a ...

... a word (as embodying an idea), a statement, a speech.

INTERNAL

An existing or situated within the limits or surface of something: such as near the inside of the body.

ETERNAL

Lasting or existing forever; without end or beginning.

My Definitions

The onion is an antibiotic plant that has been tested for healing for all kind of illnesses. In literature, it is used as metaphor for uncovering the truth or its layers often representing levels of in an event or plot.

Used for their, protections, symbolism of eternity and great taste, onions is one of those ingredients in lasagna that ties the whole dish together. The prophetic idea is the onion for your book given by God.

No wonder the Bible says;

"We remember the fish, which we did eat in Egypt freely; the cucumbers, and the melons, and the leeks, and the onions, and the garlick." (Numbers 11:5 KJV)

The following are my definitions of a prophetic idea (the onion) and strategy using lasagna.

PROPHETIC IDEA

- God The Creator, and the Word or idea that comes from Him to produce and volunteer the imagined framework's delivery.
- Words become the strategic framework in writing your book. Purposeful writing draws from the idea and applies it strategically.

LASAGNA STRATEGY

- A wave of layers uniquely built in the interest of others to enjoy.
- A masterpiece created by the maker's life experiences, responding to life's lemon's complexity and their tune into its production.
- Dimensionally, this strategy includes thought, winning, and prophetic insight.

  Synonyms: results, operable, whole, grit, fulfillment, delineation, design, tactics, recipe, illustration, performance, delivery, inventive, imaginative, ingenuity.

Here are a few strategies to help your writing journey, whether it is your first or 25th book.

#1 Noodle Strategy (An eternal, not internal perspective)

Write from the base of the noodle.

In my book, Life Through Lasagna Eyes: The Recipes for Life, I explain how noodles provide the groundwork for building unique lasagnas. It might sound strange to write from a noodle base; but, your prophetic idea needs a platform for your seed to grow when launching.

When writing from the base through an eternal perspective lens, here are a few things to do:

- Take out time to hear and listen to the idea prophetically.
- Meditate on the prophetic idea (discussed more in Part 2).
- Dust off your calculator or purchase a new one. It will be a handy tool later in this manual.

#2 Ingredient Strategy (Production)

Layer your words

Using the base noodle, write the ingredients between the noodles. Always question your truths and values about your passion. Define the message that is inside of you waiting to come out.

Maybe you have imagined influencing behavior or culture, introducing a new idea, motivating a city or baseball team. You have a story inside you that is longing to be layered. The challenge may be how, what, and where to begin. Those are all healthy challenges.

A fantastic place to start is not only from your journal writings but by leaning into the pantry of your imagination. What does it sound like, how it performs, describe the atmosphere, is there an aroma? Fully illustrate it! Your dreams, hopes, experiences, coupled with prophetic insight, are the ingredients nestled between the layers of your noodle/base. Nestling those ingredients, no matter the complexity, positions you for the baking strategy you need for your target audience to enjoy. Think of it this way, when you lean on an object, an indentation is left. You want the reader to feel the invisible blueprint of your impressions as they read.

#3 Baking Strategy (Enhancement)

The ingredients and noodles are joining together and expanding.

Enhancement

- An add on or improvement that makes something better.
- An increase of improvement in quality, value, or extent.
- To raise to a higher degree, intensity, magnify, elevate, upgrade, enlarge, reinforce, boost, aggrandize, exalt small, build-up.

When lasagna is baking, the ingredients snuggle together from the heat inside the oven. No one wants to eat lasagna raw; you must bake it! Once baked, the lasagna has improved in quality, value, and extent. Others enjoy the splendor of its aroma, unfolding the layers of ingredients with each bite, and the instrument strings ouie-goiue cheese when lifting it from underneath the base noodle. See how it all dances together.

- Your writing in the baking process enhances the following for the reader.
- Their taste of your book.
- Their laughter.
- Their inspiration to write a book.

- Anticipation built to cozy up with a blanket.
- A profound look into themselves.
- The sound your cheese made from your book.
- The enjoyment of lasagna with friends while discussing your book.

#4 Your Slice of Lasagna Strategy (The Marketing Plan)

Lasagna Pans

After I remove my lasagna from the oven, I let it cool for a few minutes, then slice, in my case, a few slices and eat with a fork and sometimes with a spoon. Others may use a fork and knife, bread to soak up the sauce from their plate, and some may lick the sauce from their fingers.

Even before lasagna comes from the oven, there is a strategy that happens. The table setting placement, lots of conversation on what will accompany it, salads, dressings, beverages; how will your table be set and the seating. This thinking is a part of my method for marketing strategy (Discussed more in Part 3.) Everyone has a plan on how their lasagna will be enjoyed or consumed. Regardless if done purposefully or not, there is a foundation on how the dish is eaten. Someone may share it with others increasing the brand's awareness; others may eat it with a spoon and directly explain to a family member how they devoured a tasty dish with a spoon. Many individuals might use a knife and fork to enjoy the layered masterpiece.

Strategies happen every day. Preparing for a vacation, meal, sale projections, purchasing a new home, and going to college are a few examples. Expanding your marketing strategy using a lasagna lens beyond your natural view stretches its reach further than the blueprint of your imagination, thus building the prophetic idea's platform as an author to augment sales of your book(s).

Part Two

2

And The Word Was With God...

The word "With" is considered a preposition because it indicates associations, togetherness, and connections. It is time to shed off the noise around you and embrace the prophetic idea inside of you entirely.

The meat in your journal writing promotes the growth of sustainable words that foster your genius. Prophetic ideas carry supreme intelligence. There is no need to worry about competing because your prophetic idea, talents, and gifts are differentiators. Case in point, there are several get rich fast books on the market. Each author, either seasoned or novice, brings something unique to the industry table through their talent, skills, education, or experience.

To know that your prophetic idea comes from God is a great place to tap into His mind and explore what He wants to produce through you in writing. He is the expert on words, how they become, and what they represent. Partner with Him, and allow Him to mentor you to release a new sound and flavor in your writing. Spending quiet time and journaling is essential to build on top of the base noodle and between the layers using the lasagna technique.

The "How" Factor

"How" is a great success path question to ask! Achieving the highest honors in education, writing hundreds of books, or having very little learning has nothing to do with accomplishing success as an author or best selling author. The untapped area of your imagination opens a dimension for you to write from an eternal perspective. Not just for the moment. Writing from this area brings relevancy that brings happiness.

Your words are enablers to speaking. God spoke words, and it manifested. In the book of Genesis, God said," Let there be," and it became or was. In bridging the gap to this manual, there are many ways for your dreams, imagination, talents, or prophetic idea to manifest. Writing your book is the evidence foreseeable through your imagination.

"Faith is the substance of things hoped for and the evidence of the unseen." (Hebrews 11:1)

Your prophetic idea is the evidence that your book will manifest, but you have to do your part.

Here are some tips needed to start the journey.

- Write in your journal every day as often as you would like.
- Tap into the dimension of your prophetic ideas.
- Allow yourself to dream or imagine.
- Spend time with God. Ask Him questions about your book, listen, and follow His lead to write it.
- Be flexible. Leverage every moment to write your book.
- Extract from your journal.
- Understand that your book is a part of you.
- Get selfish with your time when writing. Turn off your phone and social platforms, quiet even your voice. Pull away from all, if any, negativity.

HOW TO
BOOK

SUBTITLE:
GROUPS BOOK IS TARGETING:
Families, Men, Teachers, etc.
Is it Happiness, Full of Joy, etc.?

The following book strategy template was built through the lens of lasagna. Fundamentally, you can personalize it and apply it to your book.

The Dictionary

Look up the definitions online that details your subject matter. The more details you have, the more you will extend your writing to the audience's reach. Exploring the meanings behind your new project is an exciting time. When writing, knowing the invisible blueprint behind it will thrust your writing journey beyond your natural view.

Document the sources of your book. They will come in handy for book information and verification. NOTE: if using other resources that require permission, follow their protocol, and ask. Once permission is granted, keep a copy of the approval from the source stored in your file(s) electronically and printed.

Below is an example of a definition taken from the Merriam Webster Dictionary, etc.

> Everett, L. (2020). Lasagna. In E. M. Roberts (Ed.), Merriam-Webster.com dictionary. *Merriam-Webster*. https://www.merriam-webster.com/dictionary/lasagna

Target Audience

Define your target audience from the perspective of what your book is producing.

- Families
- Ages 18-70
- Househusbands
- Art professionals
- Singles (parents)
- Housewives
- Fashion design students
- Curious minds

Make a note to self: Dream in your message to self! Write down who you want to present your book(s) to. Do not be shy. Dream as wide, lengthy, and high as you like!

Your "To Do" List

This list can be as long as you need it to be and will evolve. Going on a trip, swinging on a swing, or singing at an event are ways to expand your experiences. You may want to write about them. Adventure helps you to explain how you gleaned from a situation while creating characters or the plot. You would be surprised at what you will find as inspiration for your writing. This list is essential! Write down what you need "to do" to get your book finished.

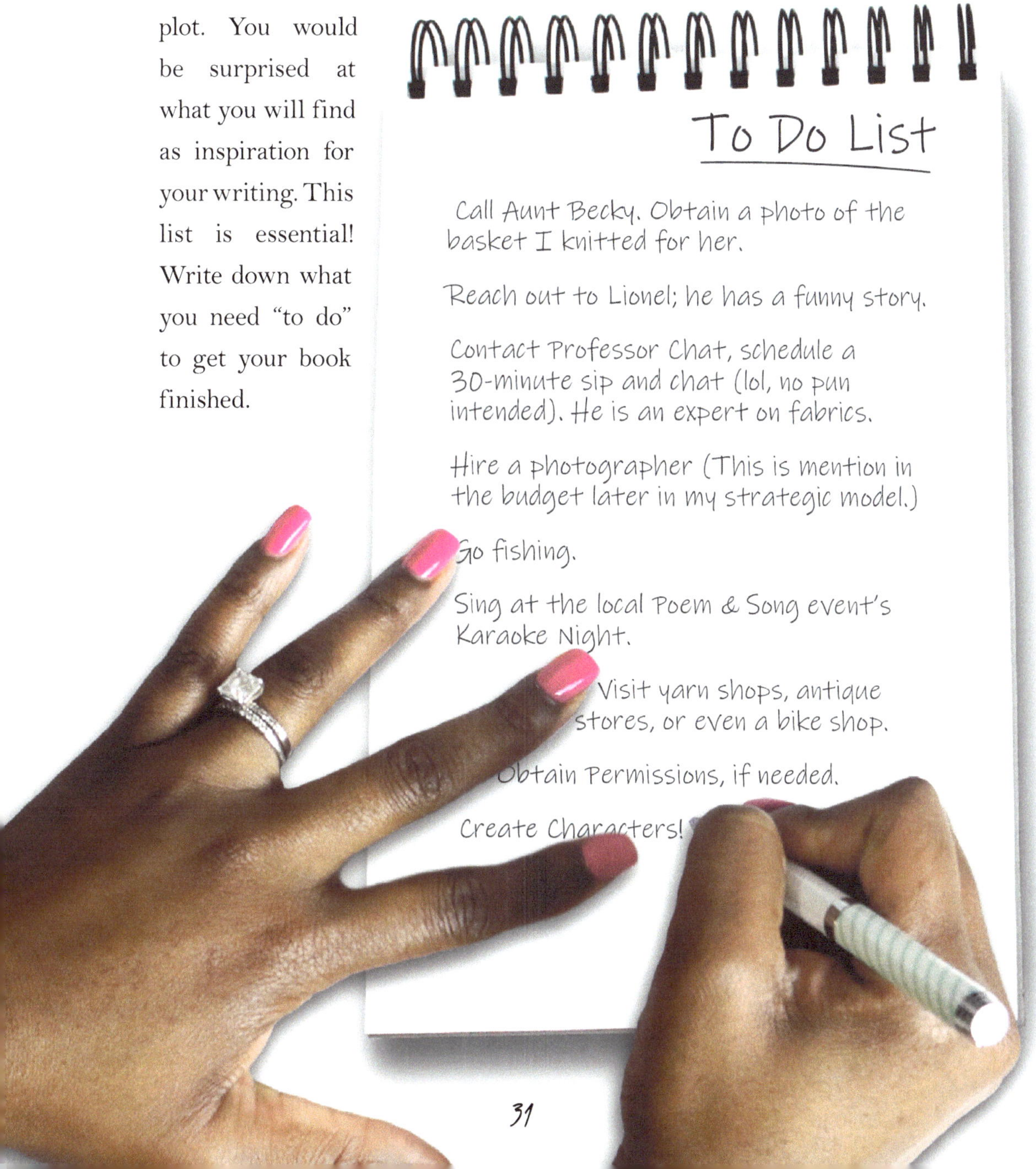

To Do List

Call Aunt Becky. Obtain a photo of the basket I knitted for her.

Reach out to Lionel; he has a funny story.

Contact Professor Chat, schedule a 30-minute sip and chat (lol, no pun intended). He is an expert on fabrics.

Hire a photographer (This is mention in the budget later in my strategic model.)

Go fishing.

Sing at the local Poem & Song event's Karaoke Night.

Visit yarn shops, antique stores, or even a bike shop.

Obtain Permissions, if needed.

Create Characters!

Timeline

Determine a release date. If you have a publisher, they will determine based on your collaborations with them. If not, until you obtain one or decide to self publish, estimate your completion writing date. Below is an example of a timeline that you can create for yourself.

Timeline

Month 2019 - Month 2020, etc.

Month 1	XX days X weeks, X days
Month 2	XX days X weeks, X days
Month 3	XX days X weeks, X days
Month 4	XX days X weeks, X days
Month 5	XX days X weeks, X days
And so on	XX days X weeks, X days

*Days, dates vary depending on the year.

Goal(s): Write one chapter per week

Detail the goal(s):

Week 8.1, create a potential publisher's list.
Week 8.2, review previous chapters and edit.
Week 9, take a break. It is your refreshing time.
Week 10, Revisit previous chapters over ice cream.
Week 11, continue to enter your personalized details from week one towards completing your book strategy.

*Sometimes procrastination is a great thing because it takes away the soda bottle cap explosion after being shaken.

Your Outline

Making a plan for your book has many benefits. Compare it to writing out the recipe for your lasagna. Now that you have spent time receiving the prophetic word from God The Father, it is time to "write the vision" and start the journey. Writing down the vision gives you direction, inspiration and motivation. Consider incorporating a vision board. In short, a vision board is a visual expression of your dreams, goals or the like, to help you meditate and accomplish those goals. It can also serve as a point of reference in developing an outline.

"And the Lord answered me, and said, Write the vision, and make it plain upon tables, that he may run that readeth it." (Habakkuk2:2 KJV)

Outlines can help you in many ways. You will be able to visualize how many layers (chapters) you have in your manuscript and define your goals with clarity. With an outline you can concentrate on the quality of your writing instead of what to write and it enables you to visualize through the lasagna lens. You do not have to spend a lot of time learning how to write an outline, but some preparation before writing your book is time well-spent.

THE HOW TO BOOK OUTLINE

- A. Note from Author
- B. Knitting Techniques
- C. Knitting a Basket
    1. Part 1
    2. Part 2
    3. Part 3
- D. Knitting Careers

Table of Contents

Below is a sample of a Table of Contents taken from the outline.

TABLE OF CONTENTS

Layout (Format)

This is the beginning of the layering process. Think about your lasagna (book). Using your outline, create a general layout.

BACK COVER For the Back Cover, a blurb (summary) is written by the author or publisher.	FRONT COVER For the Front Cover of your book you may have to hire a professional Book Cover Artist.
INSIDE FRONT COVER Be creative! Many times this is blank but you can add an image here.	INSIDE BACK COVER This can be blank, a continuation of your inside cover or something completely different.

TITLE PAGE Will be at the top or middle of the page. It includes: Your Book Title Authors Name	BOOK INFORMATION Photographs, copyrights, ISBN, etc.
A PHOTO, DEDICATION, ETC. This page is for a personal note for someone or something special.	FOREWORD A short introduction to a book, typically by a person other than the author.
TABLE OF CONTENTS Be as creative as you would like. Unrestrict your view and imagine through the lasagna lens!!	AUTHOR'S NOTE Layer yourself, experience, let your reader know who you are.
INTRODUCTION/ PROLOGUE A book description. Give us a summary of your layered conversations between the lasagna lens.	SOMETHING YOU WOULD LIKE HERE … a quote from you, etc.

Add pictures that bring relevancy to your subject manner. Remember to purchase any photo stock or gain permission from the resource you decide to use. Follow their protocol for approval to use in your book.

CHAPTER ONE Layer it, guys and gals! This is where you build between and on top of the base noodle.	PAGES →
CHAPTER TWO Build on the excitement from Chapter One! Introduce something new to the readers.	PAGES →
CHAPTER THREE That's it, your sauce is on its way; keep writing! Your reader can not wait to read about your sauce in the layer.	PAGES →
CHAPTER FOUR Well, guys and gals, write as many chapters as your heart desires.	AFTERWORD A concluding section usually written by a person other than the author.

Feel free to incorporate other pages between the layers of your chapters. When I completed my book strategy, what I thought would be about 40 pages, turned into 250 plus pages.

Budget

Every strategy needs a budget. As you spent time with God concerning the prophetic idea, listen for components you will need to complete your book successfully. Create a budget using the example below as a guide.

Items	Projected Estimate	Actual To Date
Notebooks	$	$
Editor	$	$
ISBN, Barcode, etc.	$	$
Cover Design	$	$
Marketing	$	$

You can also detail the time (hours) needed to write in your budget: Project hours, then document actual hours and place them in the proper column.

Needs Are!

There are things you may need. Be generous to yourself and write them here and in the back of the book.

Sponsorship/Donations

Speak to your local neighborhood or large retail book stores. Introduce yourself, inquiry about their process for books to be at their store(s) location. Explore how to become a sponsor for an organization or company. Discover which ones align with your message and introduce yourself. We all know opposites attract; magnets attract other iron-containing objects or aligning itself in an external magnetic field. Therefore, as a suggestion, seek out other opportunities that may be the opposite.

Donations are also a great way to connect to your cause as an author. Perhaps you thought about reading to terminally ill children, adding value to the educational system, teaching homeless men and women how to cook, and more. Donate your books to organizations, schools, shelters, doctor's offices, etc. Connect with the coordinating representative, and you both take it from there. Begin by sharing your story or make it about them. Ask the representing person to share their story. Leverage your opportunities by reaching out to friends, people you may have met in your journey and asking them to connect you to an individual(s) for sponsorship. In any of the scenarios, if rejected, move on. Do not stay stuck in the "no." There are several "yes's" waiting to hear from you.

Write down your introduction, list of organizations, or companies, etc. This manual's end is layered with notepad lines to be used as your notebooks to write your unique building opportunities.

Marketing

Lasagna has a purpose before and after it is placed in the oven. I call this the preparatory stage process. Sourcing ingredients, defining the budget, and every step it takes to get the lasagna cooking. Its careful removal to enjoy is significant to the layering of your marketing strategy.

As an author, your marketing strategy begins the day your writing utensil meets its journal entries. Remember the prophetic idea and write from there.

Marketing Strategy: A plan of action designed to promote and sell a product or service. It also contains your value proposition and brand message.

Marketing includes strategy in several components:

- Determination
- Authorization
- Courage
- Value
- Faith-Place

Growing up, we heard many Bible stories. I recall the story of the Israelites that chronically complained. Moses sent 12 spies to spy on the promised land they would overtake, and 10 of them bowed down to defeat. God angered by their lack of faith and used Joshua and Caleb to return to the promised land (for more on Joshua and Caleb, the Holy Bible and other resources on the internet are good places to begin.)

"Then Caleb silenced the people before Moses and said, "We should go up and take possession of the land, for we can certainly do it."
(Numbers 13:30 NIV)

Your marketing strategy includes layers of determination, authorization, courage, value, and faith.

Determination thrusts you further in advancing beyond traditional platforms. It lands you in places aligned with your aim and jets to heights in your adventurous imagination.

Some questions to answer are:

1. How will you nurture or develop this process to implement selling more books?
2. What does determination look like for me?
3. Why is my book important?

Authorization in this marketing strategy is the results or the outcome of what you wrote. You are the "author-ization." So this authority is you. Caleb understood his authority to possess the promised land, and without fear, he let all that got in his way feel the vibration of his God-given authority.

The book you authored becomes a product in the marketplace. It is designed for your target audiences. When the audience reads your book, they embrace your humor, vigor, character, imagination, or even your dreams. If the reader needed to laugh or escape from the world, you have answered a need in their life.

The courage to sell your product may be frightening if you have never sold anything before. You may even feel like you are not entitled due to low self-esteem or even worthlessness. This part of your marketing strategy is unique.

I remember the anxiety I felt leading up to my first book promotion. My palms were sweaty. I felt like I was sinking in my gray butterfly stilettos. When I arrived, to my surprise, many had already read my book. There were several people whose interest peaked and purchased my book. Besides the delicious cupcakes by Jazz's Sweets & Eats, my lasagnas' and more, the layered laughs, love, and inspiration filled the atmosphere beyond the auditorium and pulled others to attend.

I'm reminded in Joshua 1:7 to be courageous.

"Be strong and very courageous. Be careful to obey all the law my servant Moses gave you; do not turn from it to the right or to the left, that you may be successful wherever you go (Joshua 1:7 NIV).

Here are a few pointers to encourage selling more of your book(s):

1. Make your determination as an author about your target audience.
2. Sow financially dimensionally. Support your local grocer, go a step further, and help a local farm. Now your seed has multiple purposes that can align with your book(s).
3. Invest in yourself. Spend time getting to know who you are. At the end of the day, your target audience is investing in you.

The value of the ingredients nestled between your book's noodles becomes the life source in determining the price it will cost to purchase your book(s). If you have a publisher, they will make this determination. So think about the value even before you begin writing.

Faith is in everyone. We have all been given a measure of it.

"For I say, through the grace given unto me, to every man that is among you, not to think of himself more highly than he ought to think; but to think soberly, according as God hath dealt to every man the measure of faith." (Romans 12:3 KJV.)

Consumers accessing your book(s) believe you will deliver the prophetic idea you have written for their enjoyment. Your faith in this part of the marketing strategy believes that where your book(s) are located will generate sales as an author. Leveraging book sales begins before your book is written.

Marketing strategies can be planned in various dimensions. In my case, I use what I know best, LASAGNA. Your book is unique because it is written from not only a prophetic idea, but from an eternal perspective. Layering these components in your lasagna is just one example of this strategy. I can share so many more, but this one sets the tone to imagine and implement as much as you want to create your plan. It is easy to bake when all the conditions are unhindered with lack, a comfortable place to reside, and a budget for all the ingredients. It takes faith and all the components above to weather the lemons thrown your way.

To Land, Go Beyond The Lemons!
~Samantha Peavy

Part Three

3

And The Word Was God.

Writing from an eternal perspective may be new to you. Using my technique to author your book using a lasagna lens with prophetic ideas will journey you to new places, help remove barriers in your natural view, and broaden writing greater than you could have ever imagined. Now, I am by far no scholar, neither a debater of profound interpretations. I am sharing what is within me to help you expound on building your book(s) using a different lens.

"Now to him who is able to do immeasurably more than all we ask or imagine, according to his power that is at work within us..."
(Ephesians 3:20 NIV.)

THE PROPHETIC IDEA THAT IS WITHIN YOU HAS GOD AS THE ACTIVE INGREDIENT. HE IS ABLE TO EXCEED MORE THAN YOU ASK, THINK OR EXPECT ACCORDING TO HIS POWER THAT IS ACTIVE WITHIN YOU.

In this part, "And The Word Was God," the word "And" confirms that He is the word. "And" implies conjunction, accompanied, actually, together; even, also. It connects single words or terms, universally, numerals; it marks something added to what has already been said.

Paralleling this to the prophetic idea within you, it already was with you, and your writing is you. Remember, when your target audience reads the book(s) you write, they should taste the ingredients you used through the lasagna lens.

Dreams, ideas, prophetic ideas, imaginations are all examples of what has been inside you. Pull-on those imaginations, dig deep in the prophetic idea of your book(s). Partner with God and use a different view. Have you ever traveled to the same place each day? By the 100th time, you know when the traffic lights will change, the vehicles being driven in traffic, which streets to avoid, and when the railroad freight train will run across your city. Your car is probably screaming, "New route, please." Changing the direction of your view opens up areas to explore beyond your memorized route.

The word "Was" was used three times in John 1:1. It must be interpreted here by that which follows in the statement as to the relation of the Logos to the Eternal God and the use of the word "was." It is true that the word arch cannot be separated from the idea of time, but when time began, He already was, and therefore He was from eternity.

Writing from an eternal perspective includes you extracting notes from your journal and expanding it. Do not worry; it does not have to be perfect. You can always go back and edit. When I wrote my first book, the written pages stacked almost 16 inches of paper. It did not include my stacks of journals, which would have taken the 16 inches to 2 feet.

Revisiting old journals reminds you that you are human. It may prompt good memories, laughable moments, heartfelt emotions that let you know how far you have come. There is an audience waiting to hear from you.

They want to laugh too!

A few things to remember:

1. Dedicate two or more hours per week to write the marketing strategy for your book.
2. Incorporate donations to your charity of choice.
3. Partner with an organization and sow a percentage of your book(s) sales.
4. Sign and donate books to others, organizations, or schools if it aligns with the brand of your book(s).

Cooking with Sam The Lasagna Lady

By Samantha Peavy

Hey Everybody! As promised, below are a few recipes from my new cookbook to be released this year. Cooking with Sam The Lasagna Lady has over 100 recipes, filled with clusters of themes traditionally not seen in cookbooks for you to enjoy. Dynamic fun with me, lasagnas and more. I can't wait to dine with you!

Sam The Lasagna Lady™

Cook, Eat & Laugh Often!

~Sam

Maple Bacon & Ground Chicken Breast Fritters

Topped w/ Egg (R), w/Maple Bacon & Bechamel (L)

INGREDIENTS

LASAGNA CAKES

9 Lasagna Noodles

6 Bacon Slices (thick) + 4 more

Maple Syrup

6 Medium Eggs

Hot Sauce (you choose!)

2 inch Cookie Cutter

GROUND CHICKEN BREAST FRITTERS

1 Package -Ground Chicken

2 Cups -Japanese Panko Crumbs (Opt. your favorite bread crumbs).

½ Cup - Goat Gouda Cheese (Opt out for your favorite cheese)

5 Cups of Canola Oil (Opt. oil of your choice)

MAPLE BACON

6 Bacon Slices (Thick) +4 more

Maple Syrup

BECHAMEL SAUCE

3.5 Tbs. Unsalted Butter

1/8 Cup All-Purpose Flour

3 cups whole milk

¾ Cups Grated Parmesan cheese

French Sea Salt and Ground Pepper

HOW TO

Prepare lasagna noodles according to box directions (Opt. fresh pasta sheet -just replace the cooked noodles in the layering technique below with fresh pasta sheet)

MAPLE BACON

Turn on broiler to high, on a lined cookie sheet, line with Aluminum foil. Lay bacon on foil. Place in the oven and watch often. Flip bacon after 3 minutes, return to the oven and watch to avoid burning.

Once done to your desire, remove baking sheet from oven.

Place bacon on rack and drizzle the maple syrup on the bacon strips.

BECHAMEL SAUCE

In a medium pot over medium heat, melt the butter. When foaming begins, whisk in flour until it a paste forms. Continue to cook, whisking occasionally, until the flour turns light golden brown and begins to smell nutty about 3 to 4 minutes.

Add the milk, whisk until combined. Increase the heat to medium-high and bring to a simmer. Simmer for 5 minutes, then reduce the heat to medium-low and cook. Continue whisking occasionally. The béchamel will thicken and become smooth after about 11 to 12 minutes. Whisk in Parmesan and season with French sea salt and pepper. Set aside to slightly cool.

GROUND CHICKEN BREAST FRITTERS

In a small pot, add canola oil (375°). In a small bowl, Grade gouda cheese, add ground chicken and fold with hands ensuring the ground chicken is blended well with gouda cheese.

Separate the mixture into 1" to 2" inch rounds and set aside. In a separate bowl, add panko. Roll each ground chicken in panko until fully covered. Once oil is heated to 375°, add the covered ground chicken to oil 4 to 5 at a time to avoid significant drop in oil temp.

Fry until fritters float (about 4-5 minutes). Carefully remove from oil and place on a drying rack.

LAYERING TECHNIQUE

Preheat oven at 350°

Secure an aluminum pan for lasagna or pan of your choice. With a baking brush, dip in bechamel sauce and coat the bottom of the pan.

Add cooked lasagna noodles (3 for each layer). Coat the noodle with bechamel sauce. Layer in ½ ground chicken fritter (crumble the fritters), add ½ of bacon (break bacon into pieces to add)

Spread Mozzarella Cheese evenly over the ground chicken fritter and maple bacon. Lay in 3 cooked pasta sheets and repeat the layering process using the Cheddar Cheese.

Cover pan with aluminum foil, place in oven for 20 minutes or until cheese melts. Carefully remove with oven mitts from the oven and add the remaining 3 cooked pasta noodles, let cool for 15 -20 minutes.

With a cookie cutter, cut about 6 or 7 (depending on pan size) lasagna cakes in the pan. Remove each carefully and secure on a plate of your choice.

In medium frying pan, fry each egg, not breaking the yolk. Remove with spatula and place on a separate plate. Once the egg cools (2 -3minutes), using the cookie cutter, cut the egg with yolk and place on top of each lasagna cake.

I like to mix it up a lot, use the remaining (4) bacon and place on top of lasagna cake instead of egg(s). For the displayed picture, I chose not to add a 3rd lasagna noodle. To spice it up, I sometimes replace the noodles with my soft toasted lime tortillas and use feta cheese and queso. Explore with shrimp, steak or your favorite. Feel free to share at www.samthelasagnalady.com

Note: What to do with the remaining lasagna in the pan? I use the pieces to make lasagna snacks. You can cut in squares (1") or roll into 2 inches. Reheat oil, coat these bite sized treats in blended bbq potato chips, drop in oil until slightly light brown, remove and dry on the cooling rack. Freeze for 3 months of the date made or my lasagna bites snacks immediately. ...dip it in your favorite sauce.

Fresh Pickled Salsa

INGREDIENTS

4 Med. Sized Kosher Pickles (diced)

4 Tbsp. Pickle Juice

¼ White Onion (diced)

1 Med. Green Tomato

1 Jalapeno (finely chopped)

3 Tbs. Fresh Dill

3 Tbs. Fresh Cilantro

1tsp. Pink Himalayan Salt

Pinch of Celery Salt

HOW TO

Dice Pickles, Onion, Green Tomato and Jalapeno, add to a medium sized bowl. Add pickle juice (squeezed of lime optional). Stir until all ingredients are evenly coated in the bowl. Snip or cut Fresh Dill carefully with kitchen scissors over the bowl. Repeat with Fresh Cilantro. Add salt, fold and enjoy.

Roasted Chicken and Potato Lasagna

Topped w/ Creamy Kumato Wine Sauce

INGREDIENTS

1 Roasted Chicken (skin on)

*Opt. To make your own roasted chicken

1 Small Bag - Petite Gourmet Potatoes

1 -8 oz. Mozzarella Cheese

1 -8 oz. Mild Cheddar Cheese

1 Medium Onion (sliced)

1-2 Large Kumato Tomato(s)

CREAMY KUMATO WINE SAUCE

¼ Heavy Whipping Cream

½ quart of whipping cream (in same section as Heavy Whipping Cream)

15 oz. Tomato Sauce

1/2 Cup of White Wine (your choice)

Sliced Kumato (increasing additional amounts optional)

1 Tbsp.- Basil Pesto

2 Cups of remaining Parmesan Cheese

HOW TO

Prepare petite potato medley according to directions. Slice in half and set aside. With roasted chicken of your choice, debone chicken's breast and thighs and set aside.

CREAMY KUMATO SAUCE

In a medium pot, add the Heavy Whipping Cream, whipping cream, tomato sauce, white wine, sliced Kumato, basil pesto and Parmesan Cheese.

Cook over medium-heat, stirring occasionally (with a whisk) until mixture is blended well.

About 30 minutes; however it can cook a little longer (optional).

LAYERING TECHNIQUE

Preheat oven at 350°

Secure an aluminum pan for lasagna or pan of your choice. With a baking brush, dip in Creamy Kumato wine sauce and coat the bottom of the pan.

Add cooked lasagna noodles (3 for each layer). Coat the noodles with Creamy Kumato wine sauce. Layer in ½ potatoes, add ½ of roasted chicken, add ½ fresh onions

Spread Mozzarella Cheese evenly over the potatoes and roasted chicken. Lay in 3 cooked pasta sheets and repeat the layering process using the Cheddar Cheese.

Cover pan with aluminum foil, place in oven for 20 minutes or until cheese melts. Carefully remove with oven mitts from the oven and add the remaining 3 cooked pasta noodles, let cool for 15 -20 minutes. Add remaining onions on top noodles, then top with Creamy Kumato Wine sauce. Slice and enjoy.

References

International Standard Bible Encyclopedia

https://biblehub.com/greek/5325.htm

https://biblehub.com/hebrew/3336.htm

Webster's Revised Unabridged Dictionary

https://biblehub.com/greek/2397.htm

https://biblehub.com/nkjv/isaiah/43.htm

https://biblehub.com/john/1-1.htm

https://biblehub.com/niv/1_corinthians/13.htm

Bible Hub Website

https://www.biblegateway.com/passage/?search=Numbers%20 11%3A5-7&version=KJV

https://www.biblegateway.com/passage/?search=Habakkuk%20 2%3A2&version=KJV

https://www.merriam-webster.com/dictionary/internal

https://www.merriam-webster.com/dictionary/eternal

To Do List

Budget

Create a budget using the chart below.

ITEMS	PROJECTED ESTIMATE	ACTUAL TO DATE

Timeline

Detail the time (hours) needed to write.

MONTH	DAYS PER WEEK	HOURS PER DAY

Needs

There are things you may need for a successful manuscript. Be generous to yourself and write them here.

Sponsorship Notes

Extra Writing Room

Extra Writing Room

Extra Writing Room

Extra Writing Room

Extra Writing Room

Extra Writing Room

Extra Writing Room

Extra Writing Room

Extra Writing Room

Extra Writing Room

Extra Writing Room

Extra Writing Room

Extra Writing Room

Extra Writing Room

Extra Writing Room

Extra Writing Room

Extra Writing Room

Extra Writing Room

www.ingramcontent.com/pod-product-compliance
Lightning Source LLC
Chambersburg PA
CBHW040828050726
47507CB00021B/152
* 9 7 8 1 7 3 6 2 5 2 2 0 8 *